Be Safe on Your Bike

Joe Maloney

Rosen Classroom Books and Materials
New York

Published in 2002 by The Rosen Publishing Group, Inc.
29 East 21st Street, New York, NY 10010

Copyright © 2002 by The Rosen Publishing Group, Inc.

All rights reserved. No part of this book may be reproduced in any form without permission in writing from the publisher, except by a reviewer.

Book Design: Ron A. Churley

Photo Credits: Cover, p. 1 © Don Stevenson/Index Stock; pp. 4–5, 14 © SuperStock; p. 7 © Nicole Katano/International Stock; p. 8 © Earl Kogler/International Stock; pp. 10–11 © Frederick McKinney/FPG International; p. 12 © Omni Photo Communications, Inc./Index Stock.

ISBN: 0-8239-8213-0
6-pack ISBN: 0-8239-8616-0

Manufactured in the United States of America

Contents

Bikes, Bikes, and More Bikes!	4
The Size of Your Bike	6
Heads Up!	9
Where and When to Ride	10
On the Road	13
Be Safe, Have Fun	14
Glossary	15
Index	16

Bikes, Bikes, and More Bikes!

Bikes come in different shapes and sizes. Some bikes have brakes on the **pedals**. Others have brakes on the **handlebar**. Some bikes have only one **speed**. Others can have as many as ten or fifteen speeds! Which bike is right for you?

Ask your mom or dad to help you decide which bike is right for you.

The Size of Your Bike

Your bike is the right size if you can stand over the top bar between the wheels with your feet flat on the ground. Make sure the seat is not too high. You should be able to **balance** yourself on the seat without tipping to one side or the other.

If your bike is too big, it may be hard to ride.

Heads Up!

Always wear a **helmet** when you ride your bike. A helmet will **protect** your head in case you fall. Your helmet should not cover your eyes and should not slide around on your head. The strap that holds the helmet on your head should fit close to your chin, but should not be too tight.

In some states, it is against the law to ride a bike without a helmet.

Where and When to Ride

The best places to ride your bike are parks and open spaces. It is not a good idea to ride your bike in the road where people drive their cars. Watch out for people and other bike riders when riding your bike. Don't ride after dark.

Find a safe, open place to practice turning and braking your bike.

On the Road

You may have to ride your bike on the sidewalk or side of the road on the way to school or to the park. Watch out for **traffic**. When crossing the street, stop and get off your bike. Look both ways for cars. Walk your bike across the street when there are no cars coming.

It's a good idea to use hand signals to show drivers where you want to go. Ask a parent how to use hand signals.

Be Safe, Have Fun

Riding a bike is a fun way to get from place to place. Be smart when you ride your bike, and be **aware** of what is going on around you. Riding a bike is a little like driving a car. It is best to know the rules so you can stay safe.

Glossary

aware   Knowing what is going on around you.

balance   To keep steady with equal weight on both sides of your body.

handlebar   The bar that a bike rider holds and uses to steer the bike.

helmet   A covering that keeps your head safe.

pedal   A lever moved by the foot that makes a bike move forward. Bikes have two pedals.

protect   To keep something from harm.

speed   Settings on bikes that make the back wheel turn faster or slower when you turn the pedals.

traffic   Cars and trucks moving along a street.

Index

B
balance, 6
brakes, 4

C
car(s), 10, 13, 14

H
helmet, 9

O
open spaces, 10

P
park(s), 10, 13

R
road, 10, 13
rules, 14

S
school, 13
seat, 6
speed(s), 4
street, 13

T
traffic, 13